THE IMPOSTE

The voice of Mike Benson, television commentator for the Central Independent Network, was trembling with excitement as he made his live broadcast.

'There it is, folks,' he told his viewers. 'Another human life is about to be saved. Barely an hour ago, a hidden underground well collapsed and a man was trapped under the rubble. But, in no time, the International Rescue team were on the scene.'

'There's one of the crew now!' Benson darted forward, holding out his microphone. 'Excuse me, Sir, do you have a word for our viewers?'

'No,' snapped the man, in a tone which shocked the excited crowd. 'You know the rules. No TV. No photographs. Now, clear off!'

Within half an hour, the rescue mission had been successfully completed. As the injured man was carried to an ambulance waiting nearby, admiring spectators cheered the team back on board their craft. Amid the excitement, no one noticed the flash of a camera.

The next morning, Jeff Tracy and his family were sitting in their luxurious lounge reading the morning papers.

'International Rescue's done it again!' cried Scott. 'I don't get it, Father. I just don't get it!'

'It's kind of strange, Scott, I agree,' replied Jeff. 'But if those fellas have dedicated themselves to saving lives, who are we to complain?'

'But they're using our name!' cried Tin-Tin. 'And they've copied our uniforms.'

'I know, Tin-Tin,' sighed Jeff. 'Sure, it's frustrating. But is it so important? You read the report. They saved a life and that's what counts. Now, I've got work to do.' And with that, Jeff Tracy strode out of the lounge.

'Father is worried, whatever he says,' said Virgil. 'And I'm not convinced those guys are all that they seem. I just wish I knew what really happened.'

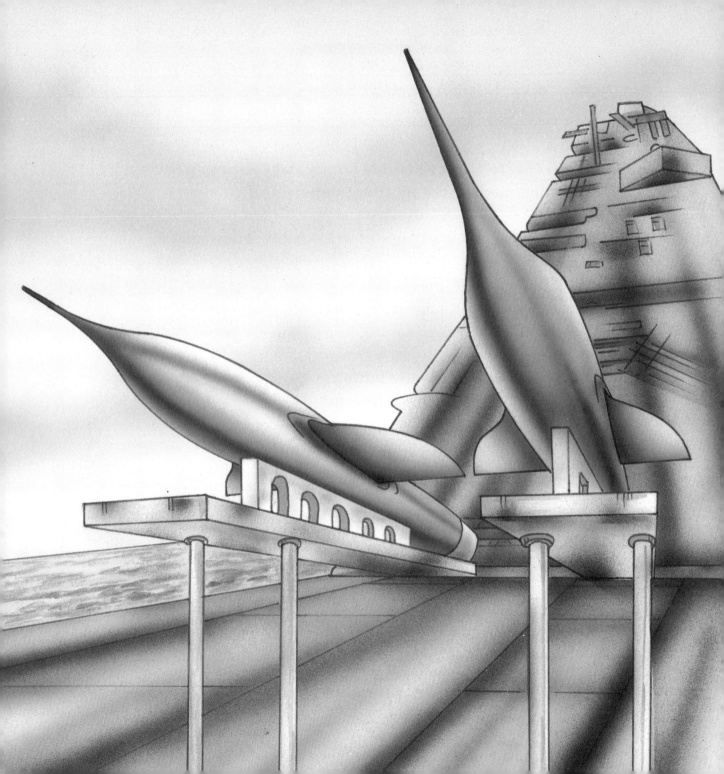

Meanwhile, at the Washington Headquarters of Government Surveillance, General Harte had received a disturbing report. Secret papers had been stolen from a vault under the collapsed well from which 'International Rescue' had pulled off their latest stunt, and the evidence all pointed in one direction.

'But, General!' cried one of Harte's officers. 'I just can't believe that International Rescue would set up a hoax like this.'

'Look, Jenkins,' shouted the angry General. 'We've been fooled by that outfit for too long. Our job now is to find out where International Rescue are and get those plans back!'

Within the hour, one of the largest ever worldwide searches was underway. When the General gave the signal, convoys of trucks set out, and probe planes and radar ships were launched.

Out in space, a specially manned observatory was set up to track unidentified craft. The message was clear: 'search and double search'.

THE IMPOSTERS

No-one was more shaken by news of the search than the Tracy family themselves. The boys wanted to set out to track down the imposters at once, but Jeff Tracy would let no-one leave the island. They must not operate as International Rescue while the General's search was on.

'But people could be dying somewhere. Depending on us!' cried Alan.

'I know, Son,' replied his father. 'But we'll just have to sit tight until we clear our name. This job must be left in the hands of our International agents.'

Later that day, operating from her stately home in Kent, Lady Penelope, International Rescue's British agent, received Jeff Tracy's instructions.

'This is going to be a difficult one, Parker,' said the aristocratic London agent as she climbed into her Rolls-Royce. 'I just hope that one of our agents will find something.'

Thousands of miles away, in the heart of the Louisiana swampland, the two men who had posed as members of the International Rescue organisation, waited in a disused mine for their next orders.

'Gee,' boasted one of the men. 'This is the best hide-out I've ever had.'

'Yeah,' agreed his mate. 'And the best deal. We make a fortune and International Rescue takes the rap. Ha ha ha..'

Back on Tracy Island, Jeff was relieved to receive the first contact call from Lady Penelope, who had been busy interviewing witnesses of the phoney rescue three days before. With her help, Jeff was soon able to pin down the crooks' movements to within a 100 mile radius.

'It's not much to go on,' said Jeff, showing the boys his map. 'But I suggest we concentrate on this area, here.'

'That station belongs to Agent 49,' said Alan. 'Jeremiah Tupple. He called in a while ago to report some unusual-looking aircraft tracks in his field.'

As the Tracy boys continued with their investigations, they were unaware that General Harte's own search was experiencing a small, but serious, hitch. Space Observatory 3 had developed a fault in its tracking monitor. Under strict orders from the General, the astronaut immediately dispatched his assistant into space to repair the faulty transmitter. Emerging slowly from his craft into the dark space outside, the astronaut pressed a control button on his suit and was immediately lifted up towards the aerial.

'It looks like it's gonna be a long job,' said the engineer as he carefully examined the damage.

'All right,' replied his superior. 'Better use your tie ropes for this. And make sure you double-check them. We don't want you drifting off into space.'

Slowly and carefully, the astronaut picked up his tie ropes and hooked them tightly onto the safety bars of the observatory. He knew his job well, but he was fully aware that one clumsy move, and he would be sucked into the dark wilderness of space.

Few people who knew Jeremiah Tupple could have ever guessed that the scruffy old hillbilly was a secret agent, working for one of the world's most successful operations. He'd once served with Jeff Tracy in the Air Force but now lived a quiet life on a small farm in Louisiana.

'Go ahead, Mr Tracy, Sir,' said Jeremiah, pulling down his rusty stove door to reveal a mass of transmitters and high-tec gadgets. 'I'm at yer service!'

'I think there might be something in those tracks you found, Jeremiah,' said Jeff. I'm sending our London agent, Lady Penelope, to investigate them, and I want you to give her all the help you can.'

'Well, that's mighty decent of you, Mr Tracy,' said his humble old friend. 'I traced those tracks to an old disused mine up in the hills. Sure seems suspicious to me.'

A little later, Jeremiah and his wife set off in his battered truck to meet Lady Penelope.

THE IMPOSTERS

One hour after Jeff had briefed his loyal agents, Thunderbird 5 monitored an emergency call. The space observatory's engineer had broken free from his safety ropes and had drifted off helplessly into space.

'Father, we've got to do something,' insisted John from his satellite transmitter. 'The guy's suit will protect him from radiation but I estimate he's only got about three hours of oxygen left.'

'What can we do, John?' asked his father in despair. 'Unless Penelope comes up with something soon, we can't make a move.'

'But a man's life is at stake, Dad,' interrupted Scott.

'That's right, Son,' said Jeff. 'But only one man. If International Rescue were discovered, it could be over 500 men over the next three months. I feel as bad as you do, boys, but we can't help him.'

However, despite Jeff Tracy's fears for his organisation, it wasn't long before his concern for the stranded astronaut got the better of him.

'It's a risk, Scott,' Jeff said in a decisive voice, 'but we're going after that astronaut. Take Alan with you and do the best you can.'

The couch on which his two sons were sitting immediately sank into the floor, taking them with it into the bowels of the island, then along a corridor until it finally thrust them through the stern of International Rescue's space rocket. Mere seconds, later, the powerful craft was blasted from its chamber towards space.

Before long, Thunderbird 3 was tearing through the outer fringes of Earth's atmosphere. Scott saw the stars, the brilliant mass of the Earth, and then the vast, black density of space. As the minutes ticked by, the boys began to despair. Then, within seconds of passing the space observatory, a beam of light flashed across their screen.

'That's him!' cried Scott. 'Take me as close as you can, Alan. I'll try and grab hold of him from the air-lock.'

Alan triggered the booster motor and thrust his rocket towards the observatory. Then, moving alongside the floating man, Scott flung himself out of the air-lock and pulled him to safety inside the craft.

Meanwhile, thousands of miles away, tension was mounting for the undercover agents. Confident as ever, Lady Penelope had advised Jeremiah to return home while she and Parker rounded up the imposters they had tracked to the old mine. But, as she lifted her small revolver into the air, a silent click reminded her of the one thing she had forgotten to do - load her gun.

'Someone's out there!' cried one of the gang as he heard the noise. 'Whoever they are, we'll let 'em have it!'

Penelope and Parker fell to the ground as the men started firing furiously from inside the mine. But, just as they were about to surrender, a barrage of bullets flew across their heads from the bushes nearby.

'The game's up!' cried Jeremiah. 'I suggest you crooks give yourselves up, unless you want to be blown to pieces!'

The game was indeed up. As the men scurried defencelessly from their lair, Agent 49 called the I.R. headquarters to tell Jeff the news.

There were loud cheers on board Thunderbird 3 as Alan and Scott picked up a press statement made by General Harte from the White House.

'The search is cancelled. International Rescue have been cleared of any association with the stolen documents and are to be given full co-operation.'

'Yee-ha!' came a voice from the back of the rocket. It was the lost astronaut who had been recovering from his ordeal in space. 'You guys saved my life and it's just great that your organisation has been cleared. We all owe you a great deal.'

'It sure is good news,' replied a delighted Alan. 'That statement from the General has lifted a lot of worries.'

Minutes later, the powerful rocket was tearing through the outer fringes of the earth's atmosphere and heading for a welcome reunion back home.

First published in the UK 1992 by BOXTREE LIMITED,
Broadwall House, 21 Broadwall, London SE1 9PL

5 7 9 10 8 6 4

Copyright (c) 1992 ITC Entertainment Group Ltd.
Licensed by Copyright Promotions Ltd.
All rights reserved

Design by Root Associates Ltd.

1-85283-780-2

Printed in Great Britain by Cambus Litho Limited

A catalogue record for this book is available from the British Library.